D0093341

AFTER

HAPPILY EVER AFTER

Mr. Wolf Bounces Back

First published in the United States in 2009
by Stone Arch Books
151 Good Counsel Drive, P.O. Box 669
Mankato, Minnesota 56002
www.stonearchbooks.com

First published by Orchard Books, a division of Hachette Children's Books.
338 Euston Road, London NW1 3BH, United Kingdom

Library of Congress Cataloging-in-Publication Data
Bradman, Tony.
    Mr. Wolf Bounces Back / by Tony Bradman; illustrated by
Sarah Warburton.
    p. cm. — (After Happily Ever After)
    Originally published: United Kingdom : Watts Pub. Group, 2005.
    ISBN 978-1-4342-1306-8 (library binding)
    [1. Wolves—Fiction. 2. Career changes—Fiction.] I. Warburton,
Sarah, ill. II. Title.
PZ7.B7275Mr 2009
[Fic]—dc22   2008031834

Summary: Now that the big bad wolf has three cubs of his own, being the
neighborhood bully doesn't seem right. He needs a new job. Find out if he
can find a job that's right for a strong, fast, scary wolf.

Creative Director: Heather Kindseth
Graphic Designer: Emily Harris

1 2 3 4 5 6 14 13 12 11 10 09

Printed in the United States of America

AFTER
HAPPILY
EVER
AFTER

Mr. Wolf Bounces Back

by Tony Bradman
illustrated by Sarah Warburton

STONE ARCH BOOKS
www.stonearchbooks.com

So the Three Little Pigs and Little Red Riding Hood lived happily ever after, leaving Mr. Wolf in a tough spot. **And then** ...

Night was falling. Shadows were
gathering around Mr. Wolf as he
walked down the path toward home.

It had been a very bad day. For one thing, Mr. Wolf had failed to catch any of the Three Little Pigs. He could easily have snapped up the first two. Yet, for some reason, he let them get away.

Though he huffed and puffed at the
third little pig's house, his heart hadn't
really been in it.

And what a disaster with Little Red
Riding Hood! It had all been going so
well too. He had enjoyed pretending to
be her granny and playing the "what
big eyes and teeth you've got" game.

Then suddenly, that nasty woodcutter had burst into the cottage and chased him with an ax.

"Oh no!" said Mrs. Wolf when
Mr. Wolf got home. "Are you all right,
dear? What happened this time?"

"It's a long story," said Mr. Wolf, sitting
down. "Actually, it's two long stories, but
I'll tell you later. Where are the cubs?"

"Daddy!" squeaked three bundles of gray fur. They raced up to him and jumped onto his lap. He couldn't help smiling, even though he was worn out.

"What's for dinner, Daddy?" they asked.

"I'm sorry, kids," said Mr. Wolf. "I was hoping we'd be having roast pig this evening, but I had a few problems."

"Don't worry," said Mrs. Wolf
cheerfully. "Too much meat probably
isn't good for us. I'll fix something else."

And that's what she did. The supper she made was very tasty. Afterwards Mr. Wolf played with the cubs.

And at bedtime he read them their favorite stories.

Once they were asleep, he made a
nice pot of tea and sat by the fire with
Mrs. Wolf.

"I used to be so good at bringing
home the bacon," he muttered. "But
these days I'm just hopeless."

He couldn't understand it. He'd
always been known in the forest as the
Big Bad Wolf. He was the strongest,
fastest, and scariest wolf of them all. So
why couldn't he catch anything for his
family to eat?

Suddenly, he realized what the problem was. He couldn't hurt little creatures any more. These days they all reminded him of his own cubs.

"That's it," Mr. Wolf said. "I've come to a decision."

"Really?" said Mrs. Wolf. "What are you going to do?"

"I'll get a different job," said Mr. Wolf. "That's what!"

The next morning, Mr. Wolf rose
early and washed and combed his fur.

He waved goodbye to Mrs. Wolf and
dropped the cubs off at school.

Then he headed for the Forest Job
Center. He took a deep breath and went in.

He sat in the waiting room. Then he was shown into the office of Mrs. Bear.

"Hello," she said, smiling. "How may I help you today?"

"I'd like a job," Mr. Wolf said nervously. "Please."

"Okay, just fill out this form for me," said Mrs. Bear. "You don't have many qualifications, do you? Apart from being strong, fast, and scary, that is. What kind of a job did you have in mind?"

KNOW
YOUR
RIGHTS

"I think I need a complete career change," said Mr. Wolf.

"Terrific!" said Mrs. Bear, peering at her computer. "I like a challenge. Ah, here we are. This one is very different."

Mrs. Bear sent him to the Forest China Shop, and the manager gave him the job. But the shop was full of delicate plates, bowls, and cups.

Mr. Wolf didn't know his own strength, and he kept breaking things when he picked them up. He did a lot of damage with his tail too.

He was back at the Forest Job Center
long before lunchtime.

"Don't worry," said Mrs. Bear.
"Hmm, now let me see. You enjoy
running around in the open air, don't
you? Try this one."

The next day, Mr. Wolf went to the Forest Post Office, where they gave him a job delivering the mail.

"This is more like it!" he said.

But he raced through his route so fast
that he upset the other carriers. They
couldn't compete and said he was a
show-off.

Mr. Wolf walked back to Mrs. Bear, his tail tucked between his legs.

"You're turning out to be more of a challenge than I thought," said Mrs. Bear. "But I'm not giving up. Try this one."

So the next morning, Mr. Wolf went to the palace, where he was given a job as a royal servant.

He was more nervous than ever now, but he was determined to do his best. And things didn't go too badly to begin with.

Later that day, there was a royal banquet, and Mr. Wolf was kept very busy. Some of the guests weren't very nice. In fact, the Ugly Sisters and the Wicked Stepmother were so rude that he finally lost his temper.

This time, Mr. Wolf didn't wait to be
fired. He went straight home to his family.

That evening, Mr. Wolf looked down at his little cubs as they lay sleeping. He was really worried now. He wasn't making any money or bringing home any food, and soon the cupboard would be completely bare.

At the Forest Job Center the next day, Mrs. Bear was looking grim.

"Too strong, too fast, too scary," she said.

"I'm sorry, but I give up," she said.
"I can't find you a job. Why don't you
go back to what you used to do? Now
if you don't mind, I've got another
appointment."

Mr. Wolf left her office and stood in the shadows of the hallway. He was so miserable he barely noticed the couple going into Mrs. Bear's office.

Then he heard something through the door that caught his attention, and he crept over to listen.

"We're really worried about our little ones," somebody was saying.

"I'm really worried about mine too," thought Mr. Wolf. He sneaked a peek around the door, and saw that it was Mr. Pig talking.

"We still think of them as little even though they have left home," said Mr. Pig.

"Last week was awful," said Mrs. Pig.
"It made us think it might be a good idea
to hire somebody to keep an eye on them."

"Like a sort of security guard?" asked
Mrs. Bear.

"I suppose so," said Mr. Pig.
"Someone who knows all the tricks
wolves get up to. Someone who's strong,
fast, and scary enough to scare them off."

"Goodness!" said Mrs. Bear. "It would be the perfect job for somebody who was in earlier today. I'll send him over to you."

Mr. Wolf smiled. Maybe there was hope, after all. When Mr. and Mrs. Pig left, he stepped out of the shadows and slipped back into Mrs. Bear's office.

Mrs. Bear did send him to see Mr. and Mrs. Pig. Of course, Mr. Wolf had to disguise himself to get the job. Mr. and Mrs. Pig would never have hired the Big Bad Wolf. But a wolf in sheep's clothing? Well, that was a different matter.

Mr. Wolf soon proved just how good
he was at his new job too. On his very
first day he caught a young wolf trying
to climb into the brick house through
an open window.

Mr. Wolf pounced swiftly and grabbed the intruder from behind.

"Oh no you don't," he growled in his scariest voice. He sent the terrified young wolf packing.

Mr. Wolf loved his job. He loved playing with the Three Little Pigs and reading them stories.

He had no trouble keeping his paws off them either. Mrs. Wolf had decided the Wolf family should be vegetarian. And now they had plenty of money to buy the food they needed. The Wolf cubs grew healthy and happy.

And so, much to his surprise, Mr. Wolf really did live **HAPPILY EVER AFTER!**

PETER AND THE WOLF

THE END

ABOUT THE AUTHOR

Tony Bradman writes for children of all ages.
He is particularly well known for his top-selling
Dilly the Dinosaur series. His other titles include
the Happily Ever After series, The Orchard Book
of Heroes and Villains, and The Orchard Book of
Swords, Sorcerers, and Superheroes. Tony lives in
South East London.

ABOUT THE ILLUSTRATOR

Sarah Warburton is a rising star in children's
books. She is the illustrator of the Rumblewick
series, which has been very well received at an
international level. The series spans across both
picture books and fiction. She has also illustrated
nonfiction titles and the Happily Ever After series.
She lives in Bristol, England, with her young baby
and husband.

GLOSSARY

delicate (DEL-uh-kuht)—easy to break

determined (di-TUR-mind)—not weak or uncertain

disaster (duh-ZASS-tur)—something that does not go right or fails

disguise (diss-GIZE)—to change how you look or dress in order to hide who you are

intruder (in-TROOD-ur)—someone who forces their way into a place uninvited

manager (MAN-uh-jur)—a person who is in charge of something

miserable (MIZ-ur-uh-buhl)—very unhappy

qualifications (kwahl-uh-fuh-KAY-shuhns)—things that make someone a good fit for a job

royal (ROI-uhl)—related to a king or queen

vegetarian (vej-uh-TER-ee-uhn)—a person who does not eat meat

DISCUSSION QUESTIONS

1. Mr. Wolf's qualifications included being strong, fast, and scary. What other jobs would Mr. Wolf be qualified for?

2. How do you think Mr. Wolf felt after losing three jobs? How would you feel in his place?

3. Imagine if Mr. Wolf had decided to stay home with the wolf cubs while Mrs. Wolf got a job. What sort of job would be good for Mrs. Wolf?

WRITING PROMPTS

1. Imagine you are Mr. Wolf searching for a job. Write a "job wanted" ad. Be sure to include your qualifications.

2. Mr. Wolf was nervous while waiting to talk to Mrs. Bear for the first time. Think of a time when you were nervous and write about it.

3. Working in a china shop was not a good fit for Mr. Wolf. Think of another job that he would have a hard time with. Write a description of what might happen on the job.

Before there was **HAPPILY EVER AFTER**,
there was **ONCE UPON A TIME** ...

Read the **ORIGINAL** fairy tales in **NEW** graphic novel retellings.

INTERNET SITES

Do you want to know more about subjects related to this book? Or are you interested in learning about other topics? Then check out FactHound, a fun, easy way to find Internet sites.

Our investigative staff has already sniffed out great sites for you!

Here's how to use FactHound:

1. Visit *www.facthound.com*

2. Select your grade level.

3. To learn more about subjects related to this book, type in the book's ISBN number: **1434213064**.

4. Click the Fetch It button.

FactHound will fetch the best Internet sites for you!